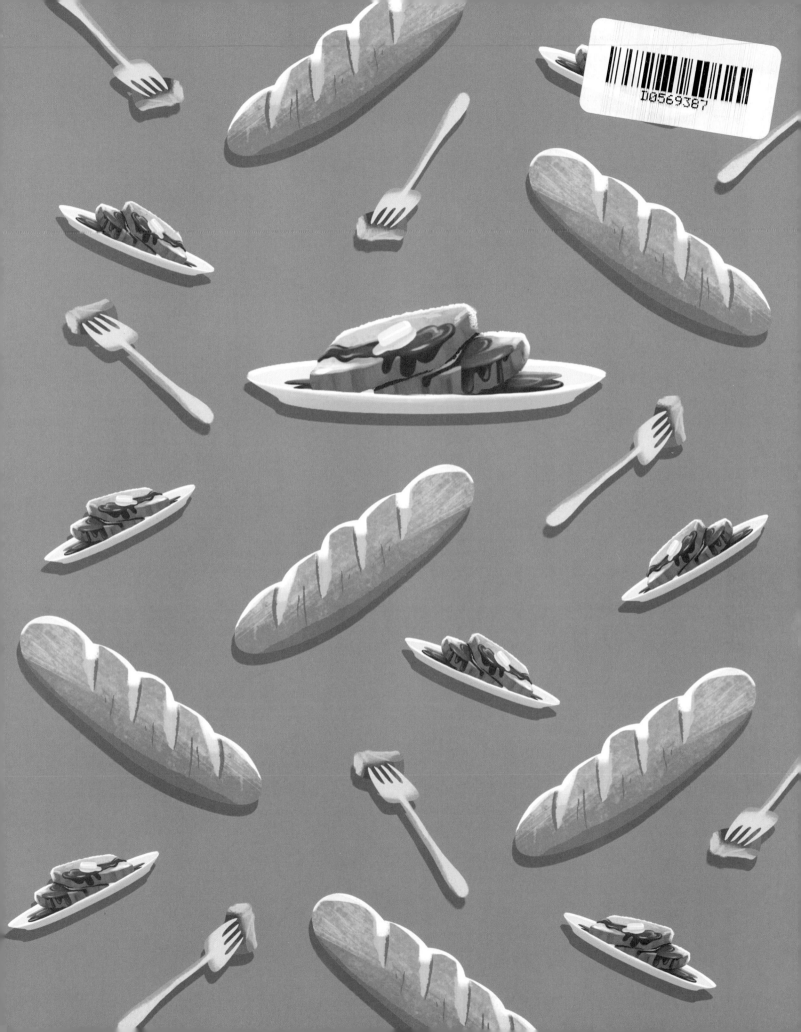

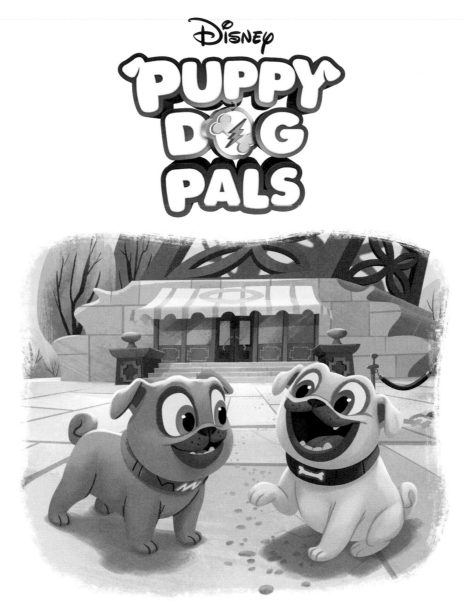

Puppies in Paris

Adapted by Michael Olson

Based on the episode "French Toast Connection" by Brendan Duffy for the series created by Harland Williams

Illustrated by Premise Entertainment and the Disney Storybook Art Team

A GOLDEN BOOK • NEW YORK

rhcbooks.com
ISBN 978-0-7364-3842-1
Printed in the United States of America
10 9 8 7 6 5 4 3 2 1

"BREAKFAST is one of my favorite meals of the day," Bingo tells his brother.

"Yeah, it's tied for first with lunch and dinner!" Rolly mumbles with his mouth full.

"Good morning, pup stars," Bob says as he enters the kitchen. "It's time for my breakfast, too. I'm going to have my favorite: FRENCH TOAST!"

But Bob discovers that there's no bread.
"ARGGHH!" he says, and lets out a sigh. "Sorry, guys.
I'm as grumpy as a bear if I don't have my French toast.
Hopefully I'll feel better soon."

After Bob leaves for work, Bingo turns to Rolly.
"Did you hear that?" he asks.
"Yeah," says Rolly. "I don't want Bob to be a bear.
I want Bob to be a Bob!"

Bingo and Rolly run out to the doghouse for their special collars.

MISSION:
Get bread for
French toast.

And the best place for French bread is . . .

. . . FRANCE!

When they arrive in Paris, Bingo says, "We have to get Bob the best kind of bread for French toast."

"But where are we going to find it?" says Rolly.

Just then, the pups overhear two tourists talking about a bakery with the best French bread in Paris.

Bingo and Rolly follow the tourists to the bakery. But when the pups get there, they learn that all the bread has been *STOLEN*! "Why is everyone so upset about French bread?" asks a pigeon. "If it was birdseed, I'd understand. We pigeons love that stuff!"

"Are there any clues that might tell us who took the bread?" a detective asks the baker.

"I saw tiny footprints leading away from where the bread used to be," the baker replies.

"We need to find someone with tiny feet!" says Rolly.
The puppies see all kinds of feet—

BIG FEET,

MEDIUM FEET,

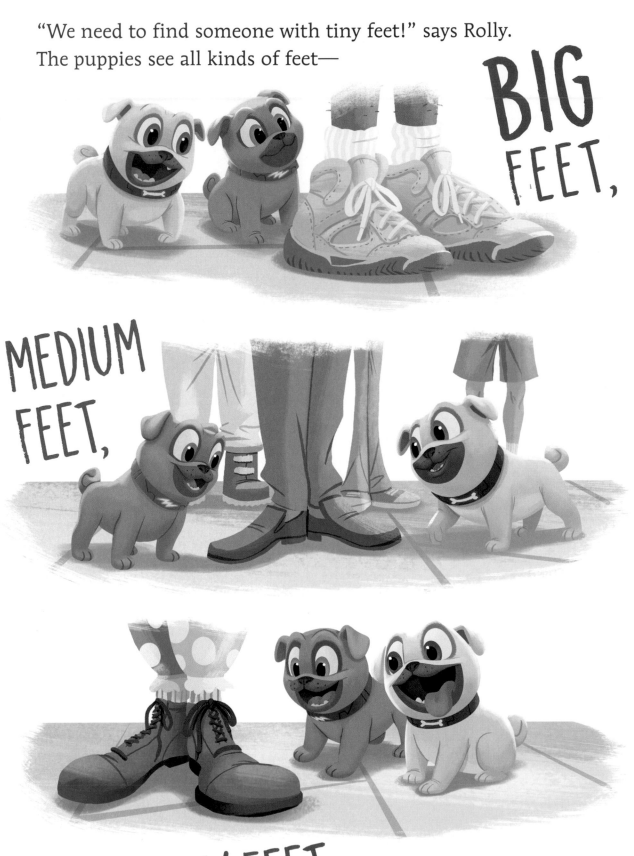

and SILLY FEET. But no tiny feet. Not until . . .

...THEY SPOT
MICE IN
THE STREET!

"Those tiny feet would leave tiny footprints," says Bingo.
"Stop in the name of the paws!"
The mice run off in a panic, squeaking loudly.
"Those tiny feet can move!" Rolly says.

Bingo and Rolly chase the mice through the city.
"If the mice get away, we'll never find out where the bread
is, and Bob won't have his *FRENCH TOAST*!" says Rolly.

Finally, the puppies corner the mice in an alley.

"We've got you now, bread-takers!" Bingo says triumphantly.

"We didn't take any bread," one of the mice tells them.

"Then why were you running away?" demands Bingo.

"Because we were being chased by two scary-looking dogs!" the mouse replies.

Bingo and Rolly return to the bakery to look for more clues.
They hear the baker tell the detective, "I heard a flapping noise,
and when I went to look, my fresh batch of bread was gone!"

"What do you think made that flapping noise?" Bingo says.

"DUCK!" Bingo shouts. Rolly ducks.

"No." Bingo points to some ducks at a nearby fountain.

"Duck wings make a flapping noise!" he explains.

The puppies begin to chase the ducks.

The ducks fly straight into a tree trunk and fall to the ground.

"We've got you now, you flappy-sounding, tiny-footed bread-takers!" Bingo tells them.

"We didn't take anything," one duck tells the puppies.

"Then why were you running away?" Rolly asks.

"Because two scary-looking dogs were chasing us!" the duck replies.

The puppies return to the scene
of the crime.

"If only there were more clues
to follow," the detective tells the baker.

Bingo and Rolly do some puppy detective work
with their noses. Soon they find a trail of
bread crumbs that leads away from the bakery.

"*FOLLOW THE TRAIL!*" Bingo cries.
"It'll take us to the bread thief!" Rolly says as they run.
The trail of bread crumbs leads Bingo and Rolly through the city—

to the Arc de Triomphe . . .

the Louvre Museum . . .

and the Notre-Dame Cathedral.

It leads them all the way to the Eiffel Tower.
"Race you to the top!" Bingo says.
"THE RACE IS ON!" replies Rolly.

On the way up, their puppy noses discover dozens of loaves of French bread hidden in the tower. But where are the tiny-footed bread burglars who make flapping noises? Then Rolly sees some pigeons. "Maybe they know who hid the bread," he says.

"WHOA!" says one of the pigeons. "You caught us BREAD-handed!"

The pigeon tells them they stole all the bread in Paris to stop people from feeding them bread crumbs.

"Everyone thinks birds love bread," the pigeon says. "But our favorite snack is birdseed!"

"Why don't you just not eat the bread they give you?" asks Rolly.

"Then maybe people will give you birdseed instead," adds Bingo.

"That's a great idea!" says the pigeon, and they all return to the bakery.

Now that the pigeons aren't stealing it, the baker has plenty of bread for everyone.

"You cute puppies look like you want some bread," the baker says to Bingo and Rolly, and he hands them a fresh loaf of French bread.

Back at home, Bob returns from work. He's overjoyed to see delicious French bread on the kitchen counter, ready to be made into French toast.

"Bob is happy he'll get his FRENCH TOAST!" Bingo says to his brother. Rolly giggles. "And I'm happy he won't turn into a bear!"

MISSION ACCOMPLISHED.

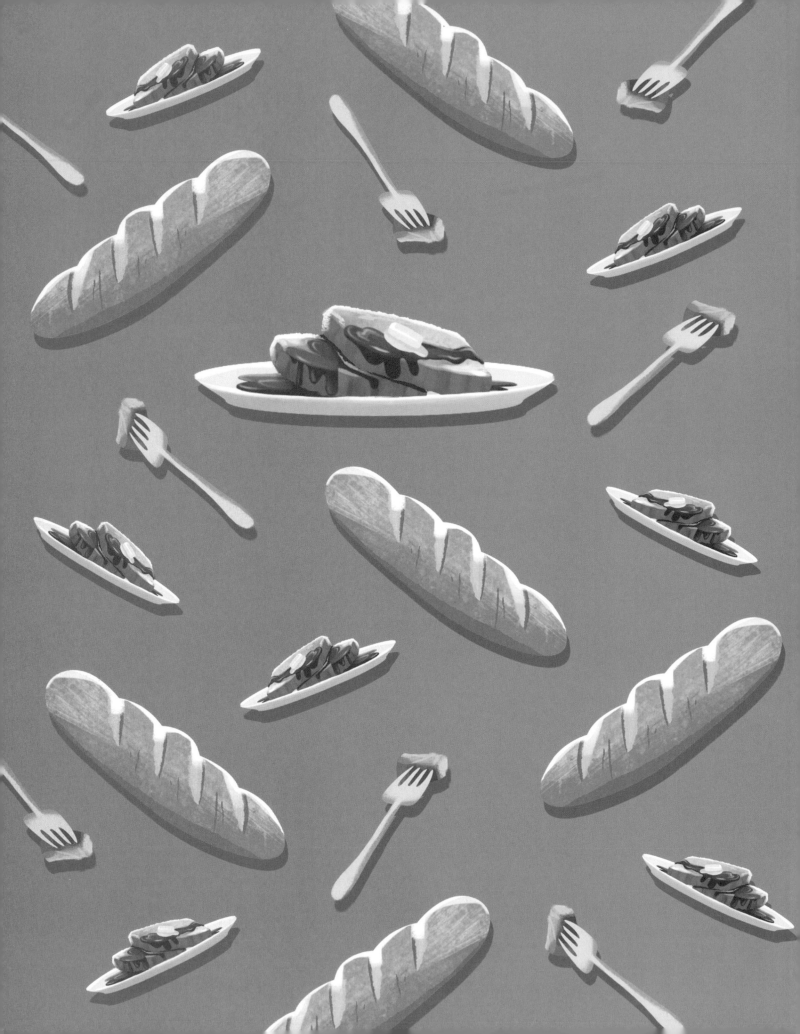